Where is My Hat?

BY MICHÈLE DUFRESNE

PIONEER VALLEY EDUCATIONAL PRESS, INC.

"I can't find my hat," said Bella.

"Where is my hat?"

"Here is a hat," said Rosie.

"Is this your hat?"

"No," said Bella.

"This is not my hat.

This hat is too little.

Where is my hat?"

"Look," said Rosie.

"Here is a big hat.

Is this your hat?"

"This is not my hat.

This hat is too big."

said Bella.

"Look," said Rosie.

"Here is a purple hat.

Is this your hat?"

"My hat **is** purple," said Bella.

"Where is the purple hat?"

"Look up on the couch," said Rosie.

"Oh," said Bella.

"Here is my hat!"